ECLAIR
Goes to
STELLA's

Book One
in the Eclair Series

Michelle Weidenbenner

by M. Weidenbenner

Illustrated by Melody Duval

Random Publishing, LLC
Random for Kids

To Alanna and Addison – who inspired this series

This is a work of fiction. All characters, events, places, names, businesses, and organizations were either derived from the author's imagination or are used fictitiously. Any resemblance to actual persons, events, places, names, businesses or organizations is purely coincidental.

Published by Random Publishing, LLC.

Text copyright 2014 by Michelle Weidenbenner
Illustrations copyright 2014 by Melody DuVal

Printed in the United States of America

SUMMARY: a young girl must live with her eccentric grandma on a farm when her mother becomes ill and her father leaves to find a new job.

ISBN 978-1-5006760-1-8
ISBN 10: 1500676012

Other books in the series
Coming soon:

Éclair Meets a Gypsy
Éclair Goes Geocaching
Éclair in the Show Ring

Chapter One - Getting the News

My name is E. Clair. The E stands for Emily, but my dad calls me Éclair. He says éclairs are like donuts, soft and sweet, just like me. And their insides are yellow like the color of my hair.

Dad called me Éclair the day Mom left. He said, "Éclair, you have to go live with your grandma for a while."

It was summer and Meggie, my two-year-old sister, and I couldn't go swimming at Abby's house. Abby was my BFF. (That means best friends forever.) Mom had always gone with us on Saturdays. But not that day. Dad was in charge, so that meant everything changed.

When Mom left we were standing in the kitchen. Aunt Sarah took Mom's suitcase and waited in the car to take her to the airport. Mom hugged and kissed Meggie and me like she always did when she went to the store. But these kisses were different. They were big fat, slobbery-wet smooches. I'm not sure where the slobber came from. Maybe it was from her drool or the tears dripping down her face. She hugged me so tight I thought my eyeballs would pop out.

Mom had been crying lots, and sometimes Meggie would see her and start blubbering too. Then it would get really loud. Dad would sigh and pick Meggie up and rock her.

I really wanted to go to Abby's house that

Saturday. She had invited a new girl, Beth, who'd just moved to our block. I needed to meet her because I didn't want her getting any ideas about taking my place as Abby's BFF.

After Aunt Sarah's car drove off with Mom, Dad dropped the bomb on me. I was going to move to my grandma's house.

"Who?" I scrunched my face, like when I eat a pickle.

"Grandma Taylor, my mom," he said.

"Why?" I hardly knew her. I'd only met her twice because she lived far away in another state that sounded like Indians. It was far from where we lived in Florida.

"I have to travel with my job, and I won't be able to take care of you," Dad said. "You'll go live with Grandma until I find another job."

I stomped my foot. "Tell Mom she has to come back home. Why did she go away anyway?"

Dad knelt in front of me and took my hand, which was not a good sign. It meant I was going to get a time-out, or he had something bad to tell me. "Mom is sick. It's going to take her a while to get better."

"She didn't look sick to me, just sad."

He gave me one of his looks like he felt sorry for me, so I made my saddest face.

That's when he said, "Grandma has a

horse."

"A horse?" That word changed my sad face lickety-split.

"Yep, and other animals too." Dad smiled. "She bought a farm. She calls it Magical Meadows."

"A farm?" I loved animals. When we had a *hundred party* in first grade, Mom and I counted all my play horses. I had more than one hundred. She took my picture so I could do show and tell.

Wait. Was this a trick? It had to be. This was a dream come true. "Who will take care of Meggie?"

"She's going with you," Dad said.

Oh, no. That meant she would be getting in my stuff there too.

But what about Abby? I was going to have to leave her, and what if that Beth girl took my place while I was gone? I crossed my arms and huffed just thinking about it.

The doorbell rang. I thought maybe Mom was coming back. But she wouldn't ring the bell. I slid across the floor in my socks and opened the door. Abby stood on the porch, wearing her jack-o'-lantern smile. Her two top and two bottom teeth were missing.

Dad said she could come in, so we went to my playroom where I could ask her questions in secret. "Where's that new girl?"

Abby giggled. "She went home. She spits when she talks, and her breath smells like fish." She stuck her finger in her mouth and did a pretend gag. "I told her I had to do chores. But I really just wanted to see you instead."

My insides got warm like when my teacher gave me a sparkly smiley face on my paper. But then I frowned. "Mom's gone. She won't be back for a long time."

"Why? Where did she go?" Abby asked.

I shrugged. "I don't know. She cries a lot." I stared at the ground. "I have to go live with my grandma in Indiana."

"We can be pen pals," said Abby. "I pinky swear we'll still be friends, okay?" She reached for my hand, linking her baby finger to mine. That made me smile.

Chapter Two - Meeting Grandma

I like watching movies. But watching TV for a bazillion hours in the car wasn't fun. My butt got all tingly. Dad said it fell asleep. How could it be asleep if I was still awake?

It was more fun watching Dad than the TV, especially after Meggie puked all over herself and the floor. Dad's face got red, and he held his breath longer than Abby does when we're having a contest holding our breath under water. It smelled gross, so Dad left the windows open for a while.

Then Meggie threw her shoe out the window. I laughed. But when Dad scowled at me from that mirror hanging on the windshield, I stopped.

Dad drove for two days to get to Grandma's house. Finally, he said we were there and drove up her long, hilly driveway. My stomach hurt. What if I didn't like her? What if she was mean? What if she spanked?

Mom said I was ink-er-gerbil. I wasn't sure what that meant. She said it right before she gave me a time-out. A time-out meant I had to sit in the chair. And not talk. For two whole minutes. Would Grandma think I was ink-er-gerbil too?

At the end of the driveway was a pink barn. I never saw a pink barn before. To the side was a white fence. That was where I saw a tall lady standing in a field with a white skinny horse. The lady didn't look like a grandma. She had long reddish-purplish hair sticking out from underneath a black cowboy hat. She was wearing pink cowboy boots, jeans, and a belt buckle full of diamonds. I guessed she was a cowgirl since she lived in Indiana—which sounded like Indians. Did all the cowboys and Indians live here?

She waved, closed the horse's gate, and hurried toward our car. "Well, look who's here! Woo-hoo!"

She even talked like a cowboy, or should I say, cowgirl? Why do they call them cow people, anyway? What do cows have to do with horse people? I didn't see any cows.

Grandma hugged Dad, and opened my car door. She took my hand, pulling me out of my seat. "Look at you, so big! Are you eight now?"

"Seven."

She made her eyebrows reach high on her head. "You seem tall for seven. Maybe you'll be like Stella."

Stella?

I must have given her a funny look because

she said, "I'm Stella. I don't want you calling me Grandma. That sounds old, and I'm not."

Dad chuckled. He lifted Meggie out of her car seat. "Mom, I'm not sure how respectful that sounds."

She waved her arm. "Don't be silly. There are plenty of other ways to show respect." She turned to me. "Right?" Then she pinched my cheek.

I wanted to bite her hand. Did she think I was a baby? I crossed my arms and frowned.

Dad placed Meggie in Grandma's arms. I thought my sister was going to kick and scream, but she only stared at our grandma.

Dad headed to the back of the car for our suitcases, sighing. "Okay Éclair, I'll allow you to call grandma by her name, Stella, but only because she said so."

Stella shifted Meggie on her hip and headed toward the house, but I hung back at the fence. To see the horse.

Stella yelled over her shoulder, "He doesn't have a name yet."

I stepped onto the last rung of the fence, leaning in to get a closer look at him. He was mostly white except for a black tail. His eyes were blue. I clucked and waved him over. "Come here, boy."

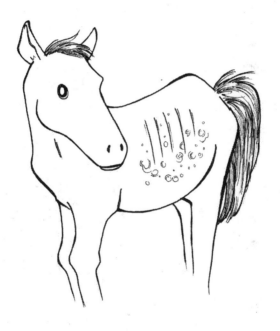

He hung his head low and walked toward me. It was like every step hurt him. What was wrong? I looked closer at his body. Bloody sores covered his middle, along his ribs. My stomach did a somersault. I gagged. "You poor, poor thing. Did Stella do this to you?"

His head bobbed up and down.

I gasped. "She did?"

Stella did way more than spank. She whipped her horse! Dad needed to know. And fast. Meggie and I could *not* stay here.

Chapter Three - Don't Leave Me Here

On the way back to the house, a funny noise came from the pink barn. The door was open so I peeked inside. Two furry creatures stared back at me. They were as tall as me and didn't look like cows or pigs or any kind of creature I'd ever seen. They looked like real life stuffed animals. One was black and one was white. They had long legs and long necks with silly looking faces. Their mouths were scrunched in a funny way. One showed me his teeth. They were covered with green and black gunk. He needed his teeth brushed. Soon. Or else he was going to get cavities. I had one once. It was not fun.

I took a step inside the barn toward them. They darted away. That's when I heard the strange sound again, a strange animal sound.

At my feet stood a large red-feathered bird pecking at the ground. Suddenly, he charged toward me, poking at my legs with his beak. I screamed, fell back onto my behind, and kicked him.

That's when Stella appeared. She reached for the bird's legs, squeezed them in her fist, and hung him upside down. His feathers opened and he crowed.

She frowned at the bird. "Drumstick, you mean rooster, stop that right now, or I'm going to turn you into stew meat."

I backed away doing the crab walk.

Stella turned to me. "He can be mean. You have to tell him who's boss. If he keeps misbehaving we'll have to chop his head off." She laughed. Her voice was loud and scratchy—like a witch. Her nose was crooked on the end too. She held him away from her body as he squawked and shook. Feathers fell.

Finally, when he stopped making noise, she let him down. He strutted away.

I couldn't move. The rooster scared me, but Stella was freaking me out. I couldn't stop shaking. *She beats her horse and eats roosters!*

Stella reached for my hand, pulling me to my feet. "You aren't hurt, are you?"

I shook my head and rubbed my legs. I wanted to run back to the car and hide. "Where's Dad?"

"He's taking a shower." She put her arm through mine like she was my BFF and led me farther into the barn. She smelled like poop, probably from the animals. "Have you met Felix and Razor?" She pointed to the two black and white furry animals. They were watching us from the back of the barn where it opened up to the outside.

I didn't answer. Stella said, "They're alpacas. Have you ever seen an alpaca before?"

I shook my head. Couldn't she tell I didn't care? There was an ache at the bottom of my stomach that made me want my mom.

"Don't try to pet them, okay? They aren't like dogs or cats. We don't treat them as pets. They spit."

That was it! I needed to have a serious talk with Dad. No way was I going to stay here. Of course they spit. They were probably afraid of Stella. I yanked my arm out of hers and ran as fast as I could out of the barn.

I ran toward the house, past our car. And went through the same door I saw Dad and Stella go in earlier. I pushed open the door. "Dad?" My breath was gone because my heart pounded in my throat. "Dad?" I shut the door and turned the lock. All the way. Leaving Stella outside.

Dad's electric shaver hummed from somewhere in the house. I followed the sound through a yellow kitchen with chickens painted on the walls. Next, I came to a dark room with brown walls. The lights were off. But the sun peeked through the sides of the drapes. Four deer heads with glassy eyes stared at me. They hung above the fireplace. I jumped. Had Stella chopped their heads off? I gulped. And screamed.

I followed Dad's shaver sound. I didn't knock like I was supposed to. I busted in on Dad and latched onto his legs. "Don't leave me here."

Dad, standing in his underwear with his hair sticking straight up, turned his shaver off. "What's wrong?"

Before I could explain, the doorbell rang.

Dad lifted me into his arms. "Who's at the door?"

I shrugged.

Chapter Four - Locking Stella Out

I clung to Dad's neck in the bathroom.

He pried my hands off and set me down. "Go answer the door before the doorbell wakes your sister."

"No!" I held my arms out, blocking the doorway. "It's Stella. Don't let her in."

"What? You locked Stella out of the house?" Dad started toward the door, but glanced down at his underwear. He ran in a circle before he bent to pick up his shorts. He slipped them on.

"She's crazy, Dad."

"She lives here, Éclair!"

I threw myself on his leg again, attaching myself like Meggie did when she sees a dog. "Don't leave me here." Dad dragged me and hobbled into the dark room with the heads.

I clung tighter, squeezing my eyes shut.

"You need to let go of me."

I couldn't.

Meggie cried from somewhere in the house.

We went past the deer heads and into the kitchen. Stella was standing outside, on the other side of the door, peeking in through the window. Dad unlocked it and let her in.

Stella smiled and tipped her hat at Dad. "Sorry, I must have accidentally locked myself out. Silly me." She came in. And winked at me.

She wasn't going to tell Dad that I locked her out?

I let go of Dad's leg and ran out of the room. Where was Meggie? I followed her cries. Dad and Stella stayed in the kitchen. Mom would expect me to take care of Meggie. She needed me. Her cries were coming from somewhere past the bathroom where Dad had been. But that meant I had to run through the dark room with the animal heads.

When I got to the deer room, I squeezed my eyes shut real tight and stuck my arms out in front of me, so I wouldn't run into anything. Once I got on the other side of the room, I opened my eyes. "Meggie?" I called to her, keeping my voice soft like Mom used to do when we played the whisper game.

The hallway was dark, but I followed her cries, opening doors as I went. One was a closet with a vacuum cleaner, one had towels in it, one led to a room full of books, and another one must have been Stella's room. It was pink with frilly hats on one wall and a small piano against the other wall.

The last door I opened was where I found Meggie. She stood in a brown crib. The sheets were decorated with pictures of dark horses. Meggie sucked her thumb and held Duckie. He was her stuffed animal. He looked more like a rag and smelled like dirty feet. Blah!

Meggie lifted her arms out for me to hold her. I picked her up and held her on my hip, and whispered in her ear. "Éclair will take care of you, okay? We can't stay here." She stopped crying and said something like goo-doo-ba-ba, and pointed out the door.

That's when I smelled a big stinky. I pinched my nose and looked around the room. No diapers here. A bunk bed sat across from the crib. The bedspread on the bottom had horses on it. Was that supposed to be my bed? I guessed so. My suitcase sat near the closet. No way! I was not going to stay here.

I put my finger to my lips and told my sister to shh. She knew what I meant because we used to play a game with Mom. Meggie and I would hide and keep quiet until mom came. Then, we'd jump out and scare her. She'd scream bloody murder. We would laugh. But that had been a long time ago. A time when Mom used to be fun. Lately, she'd get mad if we woke her up. She'd give me a time-out.

I tiptoed down the hall toward Dad's voice. There had to be another way out. If only I could make it to the car. He'd have to take us with him.

We passed Stella's bedroom door and the bathroom. The deer room was two steps away.

Maybe there was a door leading outside from that room. I'd have to look past the heads.

Dad and Stella were still talking in the kitchen. Their voices were low enough that I couldn't hear everything they were saying. Then I did. Dad said, "She's not right. And as long as she's like this I don't want her around the girls."

Was he talking about Mom?

I couldn't stand around and wait. I took a deep breath and pinched my eyes almost shut until I could barely see. I didn't want to see those deer. Yes, there was a door!

Go, before they see you.

I put my finger over my mouth again and tiptoed across the room. One step, two steps, three. Almost there. Meggie pointed to the deer. "Doggies."

My hand touched the doorknob. I twisted it. Opened it. And escaped.

Chapter Five - Dad Leaves

Meggie and I sat in the back seat of Dad's car, but it was hot. I opened the doors. But the flies got a whiff of Meggie's diaper and they buzzed everywhere. Meggie cried. She didn't want to stay in her car seat.

Dad found us. He put his suitcase in the trunk. "It's time for me to go girls."

No, he couldn't leave us. He wouldn't!

Meggie reached up for him and said, "Hold you, Daddy." He undid her seatbelt, held her, and kissed the top of her head.

Great.

I crossed my arms and stayed in my seat. No way was I moving. My bottom lip started shaking like it does before I cry. I was not going to let that happen. I bit my lip.

Stella took Meggie from Dad. "Smells like you did a stinky. Let's go change your diaper." She walked toward the house.

Meggie stopped crying. Traitor.

Dad moved to my side of the car. He knelt down next to me in the open doorway. "I know this is difficult for you, Éclair, but it's only for a short while. It takes time to find a new job, and with Mom gone, I can't take care of you. I'll see you next weekend—just seven days. Okay?"

I decided to try my emergency trick. I wrapped my arms around my stomach and said, "Bbbuuuuurrrp. I don't feel good." I crossed my eyes. "I'm going to barf."

"Stop playacting, Éclair."

"Oh, poo." I huffed. A fly landed on Meggie's car seat and I swatted at it. "Why can't I go with you? I won't get in the way."

"I have to travel this week, fly on airplanes to other states. You can't go with me. You'll have a great time here. Stella is fun."

I faced him then, wrinkling my forehead and my eyebrows. "She's mean. She beats her horse. He has sores all over him."

Dad looked over in the pasture and chuckled.

What was so funny?

"Stella rescued that horse," he said. "His previous owner didn't take care of him, so Stella brought him here to help him get better. She'll feed him, and take care of his sores, and she'll need your help."

"Well, she's going to eat her rooster," I said.

Dad chuckled again. "She always says that, but she loves her animals. She wouldn't eat any of them." He took my hand.

I stared the other way. "She doesn't love

her animals. She chops off deer heads and hangs them on her wall."

"It's a sport," Dad said.

I stared at him. "Chopping heads off?"

"No! Deer hunting. Many people save the heads of the deer they kill."

"Why?"

Dad shrugged. "I don't know. As a souvenir."

A souvenir? Like at the amusement park?

Dad lowered his voice. "I need you to help Stella with Meggie. Can you do that?"

My lower lip got all shaky again. I bit it harder. I was not going to cry.

He pulled me out of the car. I followed.

"Can I have a hug?"

"No!" After that I ran into the house, through the kitchen, past the deer heads, and down the hallway to the room with the bunk beds. I slammed the door and buried my head into the horse covers. And cried.

Why did Dad have to go too? Now Mom and Dad were both gone. And I had to stay with smelly Stella. That's what I would call her: Smelly Stella. She smelled like horses.

I stayed on that bed curled up like a caterpillar. And made up a story.

Once upon a time there was a girl who hid from her mean grandmother, Smelly Stella. The girl made herself as small as a wooly worm, curling into a ball so she could hide. Everyone left her alone for a while, but soon the grandma found her and put her in a glass jar where she could watch her.

The end.

Gulp.

I hung over the top of the bed and checked beneath it for monsters. There was nothing there but a few dust balls. I crawled under and decided to stay there.

Chapter Six - A Horse Without a Name

I fell asleep under the bed. Crying sometimes made me tired. I woke up to noises in the room. Meggie was saying, "ga-ga," and "goo-goo."

At the sound of her voice, my head lifted and hit the underside of the bed. "Ouch."

Meggie quit talking like she had heard my voice.

"What's that?" she said. The words came out like one word with two syllables. Then she said, "Shh."

I could picture her putting her finger over her mouth.

Stella giggled. "I think Clair is in the room. Can you find her?"

The closet door squeaked open. "She's not in there," Stella said.

"Not in thay-ah," Meggie said. She couldn't say her 'R's' yet.

Then Stella looked some place else, but I couldn't see where. I could only hear them moving around the room. "She's not in here," Stella said. Their noises stopped and their toes stuck under the bed near my face.

Meggie knelt and peeked under. When she saw me, she giggled. "Ecway-ah!"

I slid out because what else was I going to do? Plus, my stomach growled. Something smelled really, really good. "What's that smell?"

"Sugar cream pie baking in the oven." Stella smiled at me as I sat on the edge of the bed. "It's Indiana's state pie. After supper you can have some. That is, if you want a piece."

Stella had taken her cowboy hat off and pulled her hair back into a ponytail. She had crinkles in the corners of her blue eyes. Her hair looked like the color of dark red leaves. Like the ones that fall off the trees before winter comes.

She took Meggie's hand. "Meggie and I are going to eat right now. If you want to join us you can."

Meggie threw her arms around me and squealed. "Found you."

I waited for them to leave the room before I followed. I didn't want Stella to think I was in a hurry to be with her. But I was hungry.

We ate yucky meatloaf and mashed potatoes that stuck to the roof of my mouth. Then, Stella gave me a piece of pie. It was the best pie I ever tasted. I wanted another piece, but I didn't say that. Maybe she was trying to get on my good side. I wasn't going to let that happen. My story about her closing me in a glass jar made me shiver. Tonight I'd sneak in the kitchen when she was asleep and eat another piece of that pie.

Stella turned to me. "Do you want to see the cria?"

"What's a cria?" I said.

Stella washed Meggie's hands in the sink. "It's a baby alpaca like Felix and Razor. Have you read Dr. Seuss books?"

I nodded.

"Crias look like one of the Dr. Seuss book's characters. Kinda like a fawn, a lamb, and a giraffe calf. Goofy looking." She laughed.

I was curious. "Is it a boy or a girl?"

"A girl." She waved me toward the door. "Come."

I followed. "What's her name?"

"She doesn't have one yet."

I crossed my arms. "Why don't you name your animals?"

"I thought you'd like to name her."

I knew I should say, thank you, but I didn't want to.

Stella led the way out of the kitchen door toward the pink barn. Meggie held her hand. I followed. The sun was almost gone. The clouds were a reddish color.

We stopped to see the horse first. He walked slowly to the fence with his eyes barely open. I felt sad for him. His tail swished at the flies around his sores. He bobbed his head and came toward me.

"He likes you, Clair," Stella said.

"How can you tell?"

"He goes to you. He is afraid of most people. He won't come to me. I have to leave him his food and walk away. He won't take it out of my hand."

"Why?"

Stella lifted Meggie to the fence so she could see. "Because the people who used to own him weren't nice to him. He doesn't trust people. See all those sores on his back?"

I nodded.

"His owners didn't feed him. He was starving. When horses don't get the proper food, they get sores. I brought him here to fatten him up." She turned and looked at me.

Was she telling the truth? "Are you going to shoot him and put his head on the wall?"

Stella squealed. "What? Of course not!"

The horse backed away like Stella's voice had scared him.

Stella squeezed my shoulder. "I don't shoot my animals." She shook her head and messed up my hair. "How would you like to take care of this horse while you're here?"

My stomach got the jiggles. The happy ones. I jumped up and down. "Really? Could I brush him, give him baths, and sleep in his stall with him?"

"Soon." Stella said.

The horse made a sound. Grandma said it was a nicker. Nickers were good.

Stella smiled. Her nose didn't look as pointed as it had before. "Would you like to ride him, too?"

I wanted to hug her. But wait. Was this a trick? Maybe she was trying to get me to like her. "When?"

"Maybe tomorrow. We'll see how he feels."

"He needs a name." I closed my eyes to think. "Lightning. His name is Lightning. Some day he's going to move like a white flash across the green grass." I waved my hand in the air, moving it from one side of the pasture to the other. I climbed onto the fence's last rung and reached to pet him. "Éclair is here now. You're going to get all better."

Chapter Seven - The Cria

When I was done petting Lightning, Stella took Meggie and me to the back of the barn. A furry baby creature lay in the grass next to a bigger furry one. "Here she is. The cria."

The cria snuggled on the ground next to her mother. They were in a grassy area with a fence around them. Dirt and straw stuck out of the mother's shaggy white fur. Her baby had puffy black fur with white around her neck and face. Black circles of fur were around her eyes. She looked like she was wearing that black stuff on her eyelashes like Mom did when she got dressed up.

The cria's mother lifted her round head at us.

Stella held up her hand to me. "Don't get too close."

"Why? Will she bite?" I said.

"No, alpacas don't bite. They're like camels. They spit instead. The mother will protect her baby."

The other alpacas, Felix and Razor, were standing across the field in another fenced area. They stared at us. "How come those ones aren't over here with these ones?"

"They're boys." Stella said. "We have to separate the boys from the girls."

I liked that. I wished we could have school without boys in our room. Especially mean Tyler. He called me names like Donut Head. Then he'd laugh. It wasn't funny, but he said eclairs were donuts so I was a Donut Head. At least I wouldn't have to see him here. Not on this farm. Not in this place with Indians.

"Do you want to name her?" Stella said.

I squeezed my eyes to think again. "Star. She looks like a movie star."

"I love it." Stella reached up to give me a high-five. "Star, it is."

"How long will the baby get to stay with her mother?" I said.

"As long as she wants. I'm not going to separate them."

"I wish I could stay with my mom forever."

Stella's eyes filled with tears. "I'm sorry, Clair. I'm sure your mom wishes she was with you right now too."

"I doubt it." I did a frown. "Then why isn't she here?"

Lightning made a loud sound from the front of the barn. Stella did a gasp. "Is your horse calling to us?"

My horse? Did she say *my horse*?

Stella waved for me to follow. We hurried

through the barn to the pasture. Lightning stood at the gate. Like he was waiting for me. I smiled.

"He wants you, Clair. Look how he watches you."

"I know."

Stella bent and grabbed a fist of grass. She held it in her hand for Lightning, but the horse backed away.

"Let me try."

Grandma dropped the grass in my hand. "Hold your hand out flat, like this." She showed me how. "If your hand is flat he can't bite you."

Holding my hand out over the fence, I waited. Would he come? He did a nicker again.

He took one step. Then another. Finally, he bunched up his lips and ate the grass from my hand. "It tickles." I said. When he was finished, I yanked more grass out of the ground and held it out to him. He kept eating. His teeth were big.

Meggie said, "Me do, me do."

Stella plucked some grass. And put it in Meggie's hand. She held it out, but Lightning took one look and backed away.

"He doesn't like you, Meggie." I did a smirk at her.

Meggie growled at me and spit like an alpaca.

Stella's eyes got real big and round. Her eyebrows went up on her forehead.

I shrugged. "I can't help it if he likes me better."

Meggie cried.

Stella did a frown. "I'm going to take Meggie in for a bath."

Good. What did I care? Wait a minute. Now might be a good time to sneak another piece of pie.

I waited until Stella and Meggie went through the kitchen door. Then I counted to twenty. "I'll be right back," I said to Lightning. I hurried up to the house and opened the door. I stopped to listen. The water in the tub was running. The coast was clear. Hurrying in,

I flew across the kitchen to the refrigerator. On the top shelf was the pie. Half was left. I drooled as I took it out and set it on the counter.

Where could I find a fork? I opened one drawer. Paper. Another one. Spatulas. The next one was silverware. I grabbed a fork. No sense in dirtying a dish. I stabbed a piece off the pie plate.

Stella sang a song to Meggie. It echoed from the bathroom. Meggie giggled. I was surprised she wasn't bawling. Stella didn't know how to sing. It was a song about going around the mountain. Boring.

I took a bite. Then another. I thought I was done, but Stella kept singing. I took another bite. Before I knew it there was only one sliver left. Maybe she wouldn't notice. I covered it with plastic wrap and slid it on the fridge shelf.

Then I hurried outside again. Lightning still waited at the gate. Maybe I should have saved him a piece. Could horses eat pie?

Chapter Eight - Lightning

The next morning, I couldn't wait to see Lightning. I dreamt about him all night.

The sun glowed in Stella's kitchen and Meggie said, waa-waa-waa, because she didn't like the sun in her eyes. Why did she have to whine all the time? Stella's hair looked like a bird slept in it. Like a nest. Pieces went in different directions. She ran around shutting the blinds and talking to Meggie. She said, "It's okay. Shh, shhh."

Meanwhile, I had to wait for my breakfast. Meggie always got all the attention. I didn't want Stella's attention. I wanted her to hurry and fix my eggs.

Finally, Meggie quit being a baby long enough for Stella to make my eggs. They weren't as good as Dad's because I couldn't dip my toast in the yolks. I didn't complain. Mom taught me never to tell someone if I didn't like their food. I was only supposed to say, "No thank you," if I didn't want it.

I skipped out to Lightning's stall.

Stella said I could brush him. She had to finish cleaning up the kitchen. Then we were going to move Lightning to the arena. That's a circle with a fence around it. Where you ride a horse.

Last night, after Meggie went to bed, Stella let me take Lightning from the pasture to the barn. First, she showed me how to fasten his leash—only she called it something different.

Then, I walked him to his stall. Real slow. She said today I could walk him in the arena.

On the way to the barn, Drumstick pecked at the ground. When he saw me he charged toward me. I growled like a bear and ran right at him. He screeched and backed away to the other side of the barn.

There. I showed him! I puffed out my chest, smiling. Then I held my breath. Yuk. Farms had the grossest smells—like icky bathrooms.

Felix and Razor were out back, on the other side of the barn, far from Star and her mom. I got close to Lightning's stall, but couldn't see him. Where was he? That's when I heard him breathing really hard. Like me when I play tag. I peeked in-between the bars of his stall. He was curled on the ground. Air swooshed out of the holes in his nose. They opened wide. Then closed. Then opened. Then closed. He turned, biting at his belly. His eyes rolled up, showing red.

I twisted the bolt on his door until it opened, ran in, and knelt in the dirt at his side.

"What is it, boy?" He stretched his neck. His lips formed weird shapes.

I better get Stella.

I turned and ran out of the barn toward the house, shouting, "Come quick. Lightning is dying!" My feet crunched on the gravel drive. I stumbled and fell. My knee burned, but I got up.

Stella came out of the kitchen door and ran toward me with Meggie in her arms. White cream was gooped on Grandma's face. Her eyes, nose, and mouth were the only color showing. She looked like a marshmallow. "What's wrong?" she said.

"Lightning is breathing hard. And his eyes are gone."

Stella set Meggie down. "Watch your sister." She hurried down the driveway toward the barn.

After taking Meggie's hand, I followed.

Stella didn't go to Lightning's stall. Instead, she entered the barn and turned into a little room to the right and flipped on the light switch. She grabbed a stethoscope, that thing that dangles from doctor's necks. Then she opened a little refrigerator. "It's probably colic." She reached for a needle and a bottle filled with fluid.

I swallowed. I hate shots. Meggie clung to my leg. She hates shots, too. Lifting her to my hip, I followed Stella to Lightning's stall.

Stella set the shot on the ledge outside the door before going inside. Lightning's legs were bent under him. He lifted his head to the ceiling. His lips rolled in different directions.

Stella knelt beside him and plugged her ears with the ends of the scope. She put the round end on the horse's tummy and listened.

Meggie and I didn't move. We watched from the doorway. Lightning took deep breaths.

Stella stood, lifting Lightning's head. "Up, boy. Come on, get up!"

Lightning turned to bite at his belly.

Stella pulled on his neck.

He lifted his head, made his legs straight,

and stood. Slow motion. Stella reached for the shot and the bottle on the ledge. She put the end of the needle into the bottle and pulled it out. Then she tapped it with her finger. She rubbed Lightning's neck. Then she stabbed the needle into it and slid it out slowly.

I gasped and looked the other way. Lightning didn't move. Meggie squirmed. She wiggled out of my arms and dropped next to me in the dirt. It was too hot to hold her anyway.

Stella rubbed Lightning's neck again. "Good boy, you're going to be okay." She listened to his belly one more time.

"Is he going to die?" I said. Sweat dripped down my neck.

Chapter Nine - A Friend

"Horses can't throw up like people can," Stella said. She stroked Lightning's back, near his long hairs. White cream was still blobbed on her face. "When their tummies hurt they have no way to get rid of the yuck like we do. Their stomachs twist and they can die. The shot will make him relax and settle his stomach." Stella smoothed the hair near his face. She seemed to like him. Maybe she wasn't as mean as I thought.

"Can I help?"

Stella reached for a long leather thingie. It hung on a hook outside his stall. She called it a halter. "You can walk him in the arena outside."

Really? "He can walk?"

"Just slowly. It helps to get rid of his cramping." She hung the halter over his head and tucked his ears under. After she buckled it on the side, she clipped the long line to it. "Here you go." She handed me the lead. "Take your time."

I reached for the rope.

Stella lifted Meggie into her arms. Meggie's hands were brown from playing in the dirt. She put them on Stella's face and buried them into the cream. When Meggie took her fingers out of the goop, two brown handprints were on Stella's face. Meggie giggled as she wiped the cream off her hands and onto Stella's shirt. "Yucky."

Stella shrieked. "No, Meggie!"

Her loud voice made Meggie wail. Yep, that was my sister. Waa-waa. A big crybaby.

Lightning didn't seem to notice. He followed me outside. Stella ran ahead of us and hugged Meggie. "I'm sorry for frightening you. It's okay now." She made her voice soothing and opened the gate to the arena.

Lightning followed me into the circle.

"I need to run in the house and clean Meggie's hands and my face. Keep walking him. Slowly. If he wants to lie down it's okay. Just don't let him roll."

Don't let him roll?

Stella sighed like she was blowing out birthday candles. She frowned at Meggie. My sister kept crying. Bubbles were coming out of her nose. Gross. And I think she had another dirty diaper. Phew! The flies followed them toward the house.

Lightning froze. He stared at the ground. His tail went up in the air. I put my ear on his tummy. No sounds. What was I supposed to hear anyway? He turned his head toward his other side, staring at his tummy.

Poor thing.

Suddenly, his front legs folded in. Then his back legs bent. He stared into space. Like a domino, he dropped on his side into the dirt. Oh, no! He swung his legs in the air. Was he going to roll? What was I supposed to do?

"Stella! Help!"

She was probably running the water. I doubted she could hear me.

"No, Lightning! Do *not* roll," I said in my best grown-up voice. "You get up this instant."

Nothing. He didn't even turn to look at me. It was like I was invisible.

What else could I do? I danced. I made silly faces at him. I shook my finger in the air. "You are ink-er-gerbil. No, Lightning. You can't roll. Stella said no." My voice sounded like the high notes on the piano.

Lightning froze. This time he looked at me. Maybe he thought I was strange. I don't know. I didn't care. But he stopped rolling.

"Good boy. Don't roll, okay?"

The horse stayed on his side. The holes in his nose opened and shut but not as fast. He snorted. Kinda like a sneeze. Gross stuff flew at me. Yuk!

He scooted his legs under himself and wiggled until he stood. I grabbed the rope again. And jumped up and down. "Yay, Lightning! Are you better now?"

He walked toward me. I didn't move. What was he going to do? I'd never been alone in a circle arena with a horse before. Should I run to the gate? If he stepped on my toes it would hurt. I froze. Lightning made that nicker sound again. He inched his way toward me. One step. Then another. And one more. Until his nose was close to mine.

Please don't snort in my face.

Lightning didn't look bad anymore. It was like his stomach wasn't in a big knot. I reached up to pet him between his eyes. "Good boy."

He rested his head on my shoulder.

That's how Stella found us when she

returned with Meggie. "Great job, Clair," she said. "Looks like you made a friend."

Chapter Ten - The Best Day

Lightning rested his head on my shoulder in the arena. He really was my friend. He wasn't Abby, but he was better than Stella. Although, Stella was nicer than I thought.

The stethoscope still dangled from her neck. She placed the end onto Lightning's belly again. "It's rumbling in there now. He's much better. Keep walking him."

I led him in circles until I got dizzy. For about ten times. Then he stopped. Lifted his tail. And pooped. I waved the smell away from my nose.

Stella said it was another good sign. She said, "Do you want to ride him?"

I looked around. Was she talking to me? Must be. No one else was standing there. Meggie was playing in the dirt again. My smile stretched from one side of my face to the other. "Right now?"

"After lunch," she said. "After we know he feels all the way better."

"It won't hurt him, will it?" I asked.

"No, you don't weigh that much. He's strong. Not as strong as he will be, but I won't let you wear him out." She opened the gate. "Walk him back to his stall for now. I'll get him a flake of hay, and we'll see if he'll eat it."

My stomach did cartwheels thinking about riding him. We walked him to his stall. Stella gave him the hay and he munched right away. "Can we go eat lunch now?"

Stella laughed. "Sure, let's go."

When our dill pickle sandwiches were gone, Stella said, "Would you like the rest of the pie for dessert?"

"No, thank you. Give it to Meggie." I stared at my plate.

"There are several pieces left. You can both have one." She opened the fridge.

I kept my head down. The fridge door creaked shut.

"Oh, I guess there's only one little piece left," she said. "I thought we only ate half the pie yesterday. Hmm."

I forced myself not to look at her.

"I guess I'll have to make another one," she said.

I stole a glance at her. She winked at me. She knew. She knew I had eaten the rest of the pie. She wasn't mad. She wasn't going to spank me. She wasn't even going to give me a time-out. Phew!

#

After lunch, Meggie needed her nap. Stella rocked her in a chair in the deer room and sang her the mountain lullaby. I went to the barn. The smell of horse poo didn't bother me anymore. I kinda liked it. I took a deep breath.

Lightning nickered when he saw me. The hay flake was gone. I took a brush from a basket outside his door and went in. He let me comb his long mane.

When I was all done brushing, Stella appeared. "You ready?" A camera hung from her neck.

I gulped and nodded.

"I'm going to video record you." She turned her camera on. "We can send the DVD to your mom."

"You know where my mom is?"

"Of course. I have her address." Stella smiled.

"Really? We can send her stuff?"

"Anytime you want." She clipped the rope to Lightning's halter.

That was the best news ever.

#

Before I knew it, I was in the arena with Lightning. Stella said I didn't need a saddle. I was going to ride like a cowgirl. Bareback.

"Lightning is old and gentle," she said and gathered his mane in her fist. "Hold him like this." She stooped over, held her hands together, and made a step. I put one foot in her hand and she lifted me onto Lightning's back.

Wow. I was taller than Stella or Dad or a giraffe. I looked down. This was why cowboys said, *Whoa Horsey*! I was far from the ground.

Lightning took a step. My bottom shifted. "Whoa!" I reached for Stella's hand. "Am I going to fall?"

"Squeeze both of your legs when you want him to stop. If you want him to turn to the right squeeze your left leg. If you want him to go to the left, squeeze your right leg. Think opposites."

I nodded, but not too hard. Or fast. I would not fall. I would not fall.

Stella held the lead rope. Lightning followed. He kicked dirt up with his hooves. Grit crunched between my teeth. Drumstick crowed nearby. I squeezed my legs tight. And lickety-split, Lightning stopped.

"Good!" Stella said. "Now cluck when you want him to go. If he doesn't move then kick him in the side."

I clucked. Lightning took one step. Then another. And another. I was glad he moved because I didn't want to kick his side. My chest puffed out. I was riding a horse!

Stella lifted the camera to her face and clicked a button. "We're rolling. Say hi."

"Hi, Mom." I couldn't wave and hold on to his mane. Lightning went in a big circle. Stella followed me with the camera.

Then Lightning stopped. His back legs folded into a sitting pose.

Oh, no! I squealed. I couldn't hold on

anymore. Down, down, down I slid off his back, until my bottom hit the ground with a thump. I tumbled into the dirt.

Stella laughed. She had captured it all on her camera. "He's tired." She stopped the camera and reached for my hand, pulling me into a hug. "He'll get stronger every day. Good job! You can try again tomorrow."

Lightning slowly stood again.

"Is he okay?"

"Yes, he's perfectly normal."

I rubbed his withers—the place where the long hair on his neck ends. Stella said he liked that spot the best. Lightning lifted his chin until his bottom lip quivered. He drooled, and I giggled at his funny face.

I couldn't wait to show Mom the movie. Maybe staying at Stella's for a while wouldn't be as bad as I thought.

When I stopped petting Lightning, he wiggled his lips on my shoulder. It tickled. Right then I decided he was my new BFF, even though he couldn't call me Éclair.

THE END

Coming soon...

BOOK TWO

Éclair Meets a Gypsy

Chapter One – The Gypsy and a Girl

My name is Emily Clair, but my friends used to call me Éclair. I don't have any friends now because I moved a few weeks ago to live with my grandma. I hope to make some new friends soon. Maybe they'll call me Éclair too.

When Mom got sick and had to go away to get better, Dad had to find another job, which is why my sister and I have to live with Stella on her farm. She's my grandma, but she likes me to call her Stella because she thinks that name doesn't sound old. But it does.

Mom is at a place like a hospital that will help her get better so she smiles more. I miss her.

My only choice for playmates on the farm is Meggie, my two-year-old sister, or the animals in the barn. I usually play with the animals because they don't whine or cry like Meggie does. Right now Meggie is taking her nap. That is the best part of the day—when she's sleeping.

The summer's sun is out now. An hour ago the wind blew the rain away so there are puddles for Drumstick to wash his feathers in. He's the mean rooster that used to chase me until I became the boss of him.

I'm in the pasture with Lightning, my new BFF. He's a rescued horse. That means he was skinny and sick and had sores all over his body because someone didn't treat him right. Then Stella saved him. She brought him to her farm and healed him. He likes me because I feed him the greenest grass in Stella's yard and let him eat it out of my hand. His lips curl and he makes a munching sound like it's so yummy, but it's not. I ate some yesterday and it was gross. I spit it out. Why does he think it tastes good?

Stella waves at me from the back porch and walks toward the gate. She wears her jeans, a white shirt with gold sparkles and her jewelry belt, the one with colored gemstones. Stella is *different*. I think she likes to play dress-up and pretend she's a cowgirl. She has red and purple hair, and sometimes she wears a cowboy hat.

She lifts her pink cowgirl boot onto the fence and says, "Éclair, I've decided to take in a few boarders."

"Boarders?" I asked.

"Horses," she said. We have several extra stalls in the barn, so I put an ad in the paper to see if there were horses that needed a place to stay."

"But horses can't read." I said.

Stella chuckled. "You're right, but hopefully their owners can." She nodded toward the truck and trailer pulling into the driveway. "Looks like our first boarder is here now."

The white truck climbed the steep driveway. Its tires crunched on the rocks. The driver pulled all the way to Stella's pink barn and turned around so the trailer was closest to the pasture where I stood. A black and white horse with long, flowing hair peeked out the window.

Lightning trotted to the fence, his eyes on the new horse.

I watched.

The lady driver climbed out of the truck. Two long dark braids hung past her shoulders. She wore a purple top and jeans. Reaching for Stella's hand, she said, "Hi, I'm Ocean Faa."

Ocean, like the water?

A girl about my age climbed out of the

other side of the truck. Her hair was also in two dark braids, but she wore a long red flowered skirt like an old lady would wear, and a yellow scarf around her neck. Why was she dressed like that? Her eyes weren't dark like her mothers. They were blue like the bottom of a swimming pool. She held the lady's hand and hid halfway behind her.

"This is my daughter, Anselina," Mrs. Faa said.

Stella took my hand and said, "Hi, Anselina. This is my granddaughter, Éclair. She's seven. How old are you?"

Anselina stared at her feet like she was shy. "Eight." Her voice was clear and soft.

The horse neighed from inside the trailer, and we all turned to look.

"That's Gypsy Gold," Mrs. Faa said, "but we call her Gypsy."

Stella pointed to the pasture next to Lightning. "Let's let her run over there."

We turned toward the back of the trailer. Mrs. Faa unbolted the lock and reached inside for the lead line. That's a long leather leash with a clip on the end. She clipped the line to Gypsy's halter and led her out. Her hooves clippety-clopped on the metal ramp and she pranced gracefully into the pasture.

Gypsy was black and white with the bluest eyes—almost like Anselina's. I never saw a horse so beautiful. Her mane and tail were long and fluffy like feathers. She had long hair around her ankles too.

I inhaled a big breath like I was going to blow out my birthday candles.

Anselina moved closer to me. "My horse will take your breath away and cast a spell on you."

Cast a spell? How? What did she mean? Maybe he had magic. I couldn't wait to see.

AVAILABLE NOVEMBER, 2014

Michelle Weidenbenner is the Amazon bestselling author of *CACHE a PREDATOR* and *SCATTERED LINKS.*

She grew up in the burbs of Detroit and worked for Ford Motor Company where she met her husband. Shortly after they were married, they moved to the Orthopedic Capital of the World in northern Indiana where hips, knees, and shoulders are manufactured every day.

Michelle blogs at **Random Writing Rants**

where she teaches teens and adults how to get published.

When she's not writing she's playing with her grandkids or swinging at the ball on the tennis court.

Michelle is also a speaker who teaches *How to Write a Novel in 30 Days*, and *Publishing For Success*.

Feel free to send her an email at: mweidenbennerauthor@gmail.com

Thanks for reading Éclair's story.

Made in the USA
Charleston, SC
07 September 2014